Flight of the Eagle, Running of the Wolf

By Tracy Bottomley

Dedications:

 This book is Dedicated to my partner, He is My eagle, Also to all lovers of Native American.
 Also People who adore these beautiful Animals that our creator provided for us.....

Chapter 1

Luna walked slowly through the forest, The heat was so bad, Luna was heavily pregnant, she had a way to go to reach her home on the plane before she could give birth to her pups. Luna found a shallow stream, The water was so cool and refreshing as she lent her head down to take a drink, Luna decided to take a short rest. She gently laid herself down under a big tree partly shaded from the hot sun. Then slowly but surly she drifted off to sleep,

 A couple of hours later Luna awoke " oh no its starting to get dark, I must reach home before nightfall comes, She started to speed up but the extra weight of the pups she carried was making it difficult for her. As she looked ahead into the distance she could see the rest of her pack, She let out a loud howl so they knew of her arrive home. The farther of the pups rushed out to meet her, they rubbed noses as a sigh of there affection, They entered into there den for the night, Luna had a feeling her pups were to be born,

That night Luna gave birth to 5 beautiful

wolf pups, 4 were grey but the smallest one was black. The other wolves of the pack just turned there noses up at this pup, Luna started to clean all the wolf pups but when she got to the small black one, she thought for a minute this is strange both me and your farther are grey. The farther came towards mum and pup, " We are going to have to be careful with this one it seems all very strange he seems very small, this may be troublesome for the pack when it gets close to leaving home, Luna looked sadly at the farther, " I feel that this little one will be the hardest to rear and end up alone, we will see what happens, So what are we going to call the babies, in the end they finally chose names they will be Kiowa, **Lolo** , Mishawaka, and Hookah , " What about our son the little black one"? The farther picks him up by the scruff and takes one long hard look at him, well well its going to have to be, Aadvay "What does that mean". The farther replied it means our son is different there is something about him that makes him more noticeable from the rest, "now you have been through a lot tonight Luna you need to get some rest,.

The next morning the pack awoke all the pups had there feed apart from one, yes Advair. He wasent interested for some reason never hardly moved, Luna approached him and nuzzled him with her nose, Thankfully he was still asleep and woke for breakfast, Farther came into the den, Luna I must go out to hunt, I will not be long, you stay and watch the pups while im away OK"? "Yes Luna replied just becarful" and with that he was gone, Quite some time passed but no sight of Farther, Luna was pacing the den up and down rest of day wondering what had happened, " I must see if he is OK he could have been hurt or anything" But I cant leave the Pups, Mabe just a very short time would be OK, But just as this was said one of the other older wolf pack came running back in panting like mad, "There has been some hunters at the other side of the forest he said" I have to bear you with bad news, Farther was shot at and died a short time later there was nothing I or any of the pack could do, Luna crouched down tears from her eyes howling very loud for her loss, The other wolf tried to comfort her, she huddled up close to the wolf pups, now I have to bring you up without a farther this is not good at all. We need to think up a plan we can not let these cruel people get away with it said one of the wolves, We must plan an attack, These Evil men humans deserve to die a slow painful Death. "What can we do Luna asks. Im not too sure said the other wolf but well think of something, but for now we all need some good rest, Luna and her pups settled down for the night, the other wolf did one final circle of the den to make sure it was safe, darkness fell everything went quiet.

 The next morning Luna awoke the den was empty, the rest of the Wolf pack had gone. Luna was worried she made sure the pups were safe and went out to see if she could see the others, but nothing, She did one last check around the outside of the den, half way around it she spotted a trail of blood on the ground, it looked like someone had been hurt and had been dragged across the forest path, Luna decided to follow the Trail of blood on the footpath, To her shock horror she found the other 3 wolves from the wolf pack spread out across the ground covered in bright red blood, they had been killed, her head hung and she howled out and started snarling with anger, bearing teeth and all. A hunter came out from behind a tree with a gun " Now I got you" Lunar turned to run but it was too late a loud bang was heard as a bullet shot out of the gun, which was aimed straight at her, it hit her in the side of the head, she hit the ground with a loud yelp. " Got you" shouted the man. He watched as Luna laid on the ground not been able to move, her breathing was getting shallow, "that another one down". The hunter decided to go further into the woodlands and he came upon the Wolfs den where the pups were. He had a very good luck around but luckily did not see the pups and left, "Nothing left here now he shouted to his fellow hunter. So they packed up and moved on. It was getting nearer to the pups been ready to set out on there own and live there lives on the planes, but due to the loss of there parents had struggled with food water, Two of the Wolf pups were eaten, and 2 died due to lack of the care they needed, There was only Aryan left, he realised that the world is gonna be lonely wide place on his own, left to fend for himself. He managed to find some scraps of food for supper and get to the shallow part of the stream to lap up the cool fresh water. Another day was nearly over, Aryan, found a quiet corner in the den and snuggled down to sleep, Scared lonely on his own, all he could hear was a silent rustle of the breeze flowing through the trees and fell asleep.

Chapter 2

The next morning Aryan woke bright and early, looking around the den he realised what was happening, life alone looked very grim. He found some small scraps of food to eat, then he walked out of the den, towards the stream for a drink, Aryan decided he must do this he needs to set out to see the planes, He got himself prepared ready to face whatever lied ahead. He set off down the forest path getting further away from the den, he heard a loud snap as he stood on a branch, which in turn made him jump, He carried on walking till he come to a large surrounding of trees all close up together, He sat in the quiet for a while just listening and smelling the air. He let out a small howl to let others know of his presence. Suddenly he heard a loud pitched buzzing sound, wondered what it could be, he walked towards a clump of worn down trees, he used his body to shift a small branch to one side, and to his amazement there on the ground was a bird, it was quite a large bird, just laid there with hardly any movement. He moved forward to take a look, It was an

Eagle, it looked like it was badly hurt, Day was not sure what to do, The bird could hardly lift its head,. It looked like the Eagle may have ingested something or had been poisoned as there was no markings or blood to suggest it had been hurt physically. I need to help this bird thought Aaydan, but not sure what I can do, so he managed to nuzzle the bird round into what hopefully was a more comfortable position, I suspect he will need to eat and require water, Aayden checked his surroundings to make sure no one was about, looked at the Eagle and said il help you I wont desert you, He remembered how upset and hurt he felt as a very young pup, he was literally ignored and teased by his brothers and sister, and did not feel very much love from his parents. Off he went back into the forest to see what he could find. Later that afternoon Aaydan came back to the bird with some small scraps of meat he found, he used his small fangs to cut it up into tiny pieces so the bird could manage to digest it easier, He got as close as he could with the scraps and put a tiny piece close to the birds beak, the meat slid through the tiny gap into the birds mouth,

Aaydan saw a tiny movement in the birds throat as the bits of meat slowly slid down. But he knew this wasent enough he would need to get more help but when your on your own in the wilds what can you do. The day was getting hot but in spite of this work had to be done, Aaydan set off on a long walk to see if he could find more help.

  As he came to a large clearing at the end of the forest, he could see some people ahead, and what looked like some sort of place, it contained a large open fire with people dancing round it, he could hear drums been played, also there was about fifteen cone shaped buildings or homes, These were T pees, Aaydan had found an Native American Reservation, there were loads of them, also horses. They were wearing war paint and also using it on the horses too, They were getting ready for a battle. As he got closer he was spotted, One of the Native Men pointed towards him, "Hey Chief" " up there on the hillside, I see a Wolf. "it looks very young and out alone". The Indians all gathered to see pointing up towards Aayden, "he is so cute" said one of the younger children, Then the chief said we must try to get closer and help this little one out, Aayden took his chance, as they approached him, he turned quickly and started to run, The Indians followed him right back into the depths of the forest. He led them to The bird lying in the grass. Kandeen, the first Indian man to spot the wolf said look its an Eagle, he needs our help, one of the older children went to the shallow part of the stream to bring some cool fresh water to the bird, Kandeen manage to get some fluids into the Eagles mouth. We cannot leave this bird here, it needs to be cared for properly and brought back to full health. We will go back to the Rea and get a covering to fetch the Eagle back in and come back later. Then they were gone.....

Later that day as the sun was setting they returned with some more scraps of food and a small cloth to wrap the eagle in, they fed the eagle bits of raw Buffalo, Gave it tiny sips of water to drink, Aaydan looked on "please make my new friend well". We need to get them both away shouted Kandeen, We will take them back to camp, He wrapped the eagle up in the blanket and scooped up Aayden in his other arm, and set off home. When they arrived back

at the Rea it was time to eat, The Chiefs Wife
had roasted the buffalo on the open fire, she
sliced it into large chunks and shared it
between the tribe. Kandeen threw a chunk
across to Aaydan he laid down on the ground,
and took chunks out he could feel his mouth
watering at the delicious taste and smell of the
cooked meat. What a treat, "So what are we
gonna call this Eagle"? asked one of the
children, he needs a name. " We will call him
Maska" said Kandeen , "This means strong
and brave one," The children loved it so
Maska it was, The rest of that afternoon the
children played with Aayden teasing him
playing chase he was lapping there faces and
been annoyed by the younger ones, He started
to become one of the family, As the days
passed Maska was becoming strong again ,been
able to sit on his perch and fly about, Everyone
watched him sore as he took to the sky's, but he
would always return to that same perch, That
night in the main T pee, they had a big
gathering, The Chief spoke up, "These
creatures come from our creator, we are very
blessed, They have become as family to us, but
we must always remember this can not go on

forever, they are creatures of the wild, they learn how to hunt kill and eat, fend for themselves, at some point we must let them free, send them back out into the woodlands to be free". The children were upset by this, but knew the time would come and it was not far away, There new friends will be gone.

Chapter 3

Daylight came, the red started to awaken with the rising sun and a howl from Aaydan, Kandee decided he wanted to do some fishing, he got a few items together and headed for the stream, and of course was closely followed by Aaydan following him on the footpath and Maska above him, they reached the stream Maska perched himself on a branch that was hanging slightly over while Aaydan laid on the grass,in the hot sun. "I got one"! Shouted Kandeen, "only a small one, but its a catch" it would not have really supplied a meal big enough for a child so he killed it and fed it to the Eagle and said "here you go Maska it will make you a fine meal". Maska was a strong Eagle now, fast, strong would be very good at hunting now,. Kandeen packed his items away and they headed back to camp. That night perched on the tree branch Mask called out to Aaydan, please come to me I want to talk to you, Aaydan sat just underneath the tree where Maska was sat, and looked up at him, "Aaydan my friend, I need to thank you",, "you saved my life, If it had not been for you coming to my rescue I would not be here". Thank you. Aaydan bowed his head down for a second focusing on how he was mistreated everyone disliked him been different, he had nobody to stand by him or help him and this was a very heart wrenching feeling. Aaydan looked up at Maska, " I only did what was the right thing to do, its not nice been alone and hurt , you are a living creature just like me, sent from our creator, you deserve to have a chance at life, you should never be lonely or without family or friends, you never know when you may need them most".

 Maska looked straight at Aaydan, "We have a family now, and up until that you were my only friend, you gave me a chance of life and il never be able to fully repay you for this, all I can do is tell you, you are my best friend and only real friend, il never forget that and once we are free from here no matter what happens il be there for you when you need me, just howl out loud and call my name, I will sore with the wind to be beside you, through troubles and danger and il never forget you.

You and me are both very beautiful creatures with Strength determination and courage, together we will share this with others to help them survive in this life we have." From that day onwards the pair were always together, And if not they knew all they needed to do was call out for each other,.

 The next day Aaydan was woke up by some silent drumming. The sound of drumming could only mean one thing. He made his way across the Rex to where the Chiefs Teepee was, sat by the entrance and howled, The chief awoke and went out to see what was going on, he heard the silent drumming and called out to the tribe we need to gather as soon as possible I hear drums of war, Aaydan ran back to Maska and howled up to the branch where he was perched, He awoke and his eyes moved around fast focusing on his surroundings, Maska looked down at Aaydan and said I need to fly over the enemy Rex see what is happening, then he took off, Aaydan made his way over to join the rest of the tribe, The chief lifted the pipe of peace, the Indians all sat around in a circle around a hot blazing fire, passing the pipe from one and other, The smoke prude out,

The natives waved the smoke over each other as a sign of protection,. The chief spoke , There is about to be war, Maska has gone over the hill to get a better idea of what is happening, We must prepare hide all our women and children, get the horses out, Make sure we are prepared for whats to come.

 Then came back Maska, I have news they are planning on war on our camp they are not coming for food and belongings they come for your blood, They plan there ascend on our Rex Tomorrow. Now we must plan and be ready tonight, I will stay perched on the branch of the tree and keep you informed of what I see, with that he was gone, the chief said war it is. We will be ready for there arrival, lets be ready for them.

 The next morning the drums had become significantly louder. The Indians were preparing, putting war paint upon their horses, and on themselves, saying farewell to there wives and children, not knowing what may lie ahead, They prepared there bow and arrows and loaded their horses up, they gathered around the fire chanting a war dance and singing, asking for protection from their creator, Kandee placed two significant red stripes down his left cheek he wanted to stand out and also protect his people from the enemy. The enemy tribe started to make there way through the forest at the other side of the woodland, they had to come across the stream. They were a nasty tribe had no mercy, they just wanted to kill everything that got in their way. People animals bloodshed, they walked onto the edge of the plain arrows shouting, soon as Maska swooped down at one of the enemies and scraped the top of his head left him with blood running down his face. The man screamed out, he grabbed his bow and arrow and tried to fire his arrow at Maska but luckily he missed, Maska flew back to let his Rea know they were coming, The Indians jumped on their horses said goodbye to their families and galloped off towards the plain, The Chief saw the enemy. Charge shouted, The tribes charged straight at each other, arrows were flying, Indians and horses been thrown to the ground, Then Aayden heard a quiet cry for help by the river, he ran over to see, Kandees had been hit in the chest with an arrow, he was bleeding badly, Aayden cried out loud, Maska swooped down from the sky, Kandees has been hurt bad go get help with that Maska had gone, Aayden stayed with Kandees, it was his next special friend, He could not leave him to die, he remembered when he was in need and they came to his rescue and now it was his time to return the favour, The fighting was bad, buffalo killed, Indians body's laid on the ground, Aayden was licking Kandees face trying to keep him awake, he was helpless he could not do more, He just laid with him hoping help would soon arrive. Then high in the clouds came Maska followed closely by some of the other Indians from their Rex They ran over to Kandee, quick I have some rags to cover the wound get some cool water from the stream so we can clean the wound, They managed to get the arrow out and out pressure on to stop the bleeding, but Kandee was weak, they needed to get him back to camp so they can treat him better, They managed to lift him up onto the back of a horse, They set off back trails of blood and destruction everywhere t pees torn down bodies covering the ground, Aayden and Maska followed close behind, When they arrived back, They managed to clean Kandees

up and put clean covering over the injury.
Chapter 4

That evening the Tribe sat around the campfire
and Maska watched on from a tree branch,
Aayden would not leave Kandee side, He was
very protective over him, looking out for
anyone who may be a threat to him during his
recovery, Kandees opened his eyes, he gently
put his hand out to stroke Aayden, he nuzzled
his hand, Kandee wanted to try and eat a little,
The tribe had just been cooking some Buffalo
over the open fire. One of the younger
members came in he brought with him some
small pieces of the hot tasty buffalo meat,
Kandee grabbed for the meat, and managed to
eat a little, then he passed a small chunk to
Aayden, He looked Aayden in the eye and said
you are my friend, a true hero, you saved my
life, A tear formed in the eye of Aayden, as he
knew deep down he was not the one who
should be getting all the praise, It was Maska
that flew back to the Rea to get the others, Just
then they heard ruffling outside, It was Maska,
he had come to settle for the night with his
friends, and thats what they did, feeling happy.

The next day the sun shone brightly, Maska was perched on his favourite tree branch, Aayden walked by the cool stream lapping up the cold refreshing water, Kandee was feeling a lot better today but will be left with a nasty scar for the rest of his life, he managed to sit up fully and Aayden came into the tpee jumped up and started licking his face. Kandee laughed, listen I must say this said Kandee, I am to be wed, it was arranged by our Chief some time ago, I need to thank you and Maska for saving my life, you will be beside me when we marry, as a true warrior, and Maska too. You have become a great help to my people and part of our family, you are welcome to stay with us for good, We are going to make you our mascots, We will have the head of the wolf and Eagle engraved on our tools sheilds and so on in memory of what you have done for us, we cant thank you both enough, Aayden bowed his head, feeling a little shy at this, Maska stood true and proud, Kandee managed to slowly get up from his bed and walk outside into open air. Feeling ready to face them all once again after his ordeal, he looked at Aayden and Maska. Thankyou my friends I love you both always.

A week passed and it finally was the day of the big wedding Kandeen was feeling a little apprehensive about the whole thing, He combed his hair long and straight and placed on his best bone vest, Suddenly one of Maskas large brown Eagle feathers fell to the ground, Kandeen took the feather and olaced it it into his hair, I will wear this with pride my feathered friend, Then the Drums started playing and everyone was chanting, The Cheif called to Kandeen to come out, Aayden and Maska came right behind, Aayden was wearing a coller that Kandeen made for him especially for the wedding, and walked with his head held high, I am proud to have you both at my side on this special day, Then out of another T pee came Kandeens bride. A beautiful lady named Aponi wich means butterfly in the Native Language, long dark hair glowing brown eyes, Aponi walked slowly towards Kandeen smily at him, They stood faceing each other and held hands, Aayden stood beside Kandeen and Maska was perched on a pole near Aponi. Everyone was happy, The Cheif did the ceromonel chanting and prayers to join the couple together. Aayden let out a howl and

Maska, Squawked very loud making sure he was heard, all the tribe roared with laughter, Kandeen and his new bride Aponi shared a kiss, everyone clapped there hands with joy, Aponi bent down to pet Aayden. He cowered, oh don't worry I am your friend I will not hurt you, you are both to come and stay with us in our place, Aayden loved that idea, and Maska looked across and seemed very calm. The wedding went on late into the night, Dancing eating festivities, drums. Aayden and Maska followed them back to the T pee, Kandeen took his bride in and they settled down for the night, Aayden looked up at Maska you really are my special friend id be lost without you honestly, Maska replied you saved me when I was ill you help bring me back, fit and healthy, I will always love n respect you for that, that is what we did for this Tribe and Kandeen. We made him well. The moral is if you help others. In times of need they will help you, this is how you make good friendships and gain peoples trust, with that they said goodnight, wondering what there next adventure will bring.